KU-024-247

Contents

CHAPTER ONE
Hot Stuff

I t was impossible to ignore them. No matter where you looked at the 1997 Brit Awards for music, there were the Spice Girls. The performance of their next single 'Who Do You Think You Are?' to open the awards – and especially the Union Flag dress worn by Geri Halliwell – stole all the following day's headlines. But that was nothing new. For months it had seemed that you couldn't pick up a newspaper without reading about the group, while their pictures were spread across countless pages.

However, the Spice Girls weren't at the ceremony merely as performers. They were also there to collect two Brits – the best single award for 'Wannabe' and the Best Video award for 'Say You'll Be There'. They were even nominated in a further two categories – Best Band and Best Newcomer. There could be no greater recognition of the astonishing Girl Power phenomenon which had swept Britain first and now the rest of the world.

While the superstars at the awards included Elton John, Diana Ross and the Manic Street Preachers, everyone wanted to meet the girls and congratulate them on their success. Many of those who did were in for a surprise, as Geri later revealed. 'Everyone's coming up to us saying, "Welcome to your first Brits", but we were actually here last year,' she said. 'We were on the very last table at the very back, and no one knew us from the wallpaper.'

Victoria Adams agreed. 'Last year we came to the Brits just as guests. We were nobodies then, but now we're performing and part of the show.' It was as if none of the girls could quite believe what had happened to them.

But that was hardly surprising. Only eight months before they stood on that stage at the

Brits, very few people, apart from a small number within the music business, had ever heard of the Spice Girls. In that short space of time, they had rocketed to what had once been unimaginable fame.

Even as they were collecting their awards, their first single, 'Wannabe', was being played on radio stations across the whole of the United States, where it had been recently released. It was the song which had launched the Spice Girls in Britain in July of the previous year, going to number one in the charts where it remained for seven weeks.

That was an extraordinary enough achievement for a group releasing its first ever single. But even though it sold more than one-and-a-quarter-million copies, 'Wannabe''s success did not convince the critics. Many of them wrote off the Spice Girls as one-hit wonders. They could not have been more wrong.

In October 1996, the girls brought out their follow-up single, 'Say You'll Be There'. It went straight in at number one in the UK charts, and sold 750,000 copies within two weeks. Now no one could ignore them. The third single, '2 Become 1', also went to number one in the UK as soon as it was released, occupying the spot over Christmas.

The sales figures were becoming mind-boggling – 650,000 advance orders for '2 Become 1', plus 500,000 further sales in its first week of release. In the previous month, two million copies of their debut album *Spice* had sold within a fortnight.

Girl Power gripped the nation. The group were invited to switch on the Christmas lights in London's Oxford Street. Prince William was revealed to be a fan, especially of Emma Bunton, whose poster reportedly adorned a wall of his room at his school, Eton College. Even Britain's leading politicians wanted to get in on the act! In early 1997, the then Chancellor of the Exchequer, Kenneth Clarke, stole one of their best-known lines when he said in a speech, 'All I want, all I really, really want, is a strong economy with low inflation.' The now Prime Minister, Tony Blair, included 'Wannabe' among his choices for BBC Radio 4's *Desert Island Discs*.

America was next to fall under the Spice

ALL THINGS SPICE

y going straight to number one in the UK charts
with their fourth single 'Who Do You Think You
Are?'/'Mama', the Spice Girls made history and
underlined their extraordinary popularity. At the
beginning of April 1997, they notched up their
ten-millionth sale of *Spice* worldwide. Added to
the fourteen-million singles they had sold across
the globe, it meant that all five girls were multi-
millionaires. A spokesman for their record company, Virgin, commented, 'They are the biggest
pop phenomenon of this decade, if not of the last
twenty years.'

Another book by Fergus Kelly

ERIC CANTONA

All Things Spice

FERGUS KELLY

PUFFIN BOOKS

To my brother, Chris, who would have
been much more impressed if I had
arranged for him to meet them

PUFFIN BOOKS

Published by the Penguin Group
Penguin Books Ltd, 27 Wrights Lane, London W8 5TZ, England
Penguin Books USA Inc., 375 Hudson Street, New York, New York 10014, USA
Penguin Books Australia Ltd, Ringwood, Victoria, Australia
Penguin Books Canada Ltd, 10 Alcorn Avenue, Toronto, Ontario, Canada M4V 3B2
Penguin Books (NZ) Ltd, 182–190 Wairau Road, Auckland 10, New Zealand

Penguin Books Ltd, Registered Offices: Harmondsworth, Middlesex, England

First published 1997
7 9 10 8 6

Text copyright © Fergus Kelly, 1997
Photo insert copyright details:
pages i, v, vi, vii and viii © Frank Camhi/Vision, 1996
page ii © Comic Relief/Retna, Ph: George Bodnar/4031, 1997
page iii © Chris Heads, 1997
page iv © Ray Johnson
All pictures supplied by Retna.
All rights reserved

The moral right of the author has been asserted

Set in 12/17pt Monotype Palatino

Typeset by Rowland Phototypesetting Ltd,
Bury St Edmunds, Suffolk

Made and printed in England by Clays Ltd, St Ives plc

British Library Cataloguing in Publication Data
A CIP catalogue record for this book is available from the British Library

ISBN 0–140–38812–5

spell. Yet again, the girls defied the critics and broke records to reach the top of the US charts too. 'Wannabe' remained there for four weeks, and sold millions more copies. The album *Spice* enjoyed similarly astonishing success in the United States. It seemed that all around the globe, people were listening to the Spice Girls. They were number one in dozens of different countries, from Iceland to Indonesia.

There was another record to be broken – and the Spice Girls smashed it in March 1997. That was when they became the first group in the forty-five-year existence of the music charts in Britain to go to number one with their first four singles.

The double A-side of 'Who Do You Think You Are?' and 'Mama' achieved that milestone, and at the same time made hundreds of thousands of pounds for charity as the group donated all profits from the single to Comic Relief. They were also the stars of Red Nose Day, appearing on stage with a spoof Spice Girls group called the Sugar Lumps, which included comediennes Dawn French as Victoria, Jennifer Saunders as Geri, and singer Lulu as Emma.

All these incredible events had taken place within an amazingly short space of time. Less than a year previously, the girls could not have dreamed of the incredible events which were about to overtake them. So exactly how did Geri Halliwell, Melanie Brown, Melanie Chisholm, Emma Bunton and Victoria Adams grow up, meet, and eventually form what was to become the most successful all-girl group in the history of pop music? This is their story.

CHAPTER TWO

Posh Spice – Victoria

S he is the sophisticated one in the Spice Girls – the well-dressed, cool beauty, who the rest of the band think is the one that all the boys fancy. Yet, as a schoolgirl, Victoria Adams suffered at the hands of playground bullies, who endlessly teased her about her acne, and tormented her so much that on some days she was terrified to go to school.

It is a period of her life that Victoria remembers with sadness. But it is clear that the experience filled her with the determination to succeed which eventually led her to the Spice Girls. In the early part of her life, however, there was nothing to suggest the problems that lay ahead.

There is little doubt that out of the five girls, Victoria enjoyed the most privileged upbringing. Her parents, Tony and Jackie, ran a very successful electrical-goods business, and were wealthy enough to ensure that their eldest child Victoria, born on 7 April 1975, her younger sister Louise, and younger brother Christian never wanted for anything. There were plenty of signs that the family was well off too. Dad, Tony, drove a Rolls Royce, and their large and comfortable home in the pretty village of Goff's Oak in Hertfordshire, England, included a swimming pool in the spacious back garden. Summer holidays were often spent at the family's villa in southern Spain.

From a very early age, it was evident that Victoria wanted to be a dancer and performer. At the local Goff's Oak Junior Middle and Infants School, she was cast in the school pantomime, as the only one of her former teachers working at the school today, Sue Bailey, still remembers. 'Victoria was always such a pleasant child, very pretty, not at all loud or pushy,' she says. 'She worked hard and came from a lovely family. I can remember her in the leading role of *The Pied Piper*. She was always in school productions, and very keen on drama.'

Victoria's best friend at her first school was Emma Comolli. The two of them were so close that they even held joint birthday parties at the village hall. Emma, now in her early twenties, remembers how Victoria's mum used to dress her up. 'When she was in primary school, her mum got her some grey leather trousers and shoes with little heels. At other times, she would be dressed up like the fairy on top of the Christmas tree.' Emma was also one of the first people to witness the performing talent that would eventually make Victoria known to millions of fans.

'We used to put on a bit of a show together,' says Emma. 'She was obsessed with *Fame* and *Grease*. Her mother had got her the *Grease* video, and we must have watched it twenty times. When we performed, Victoria would always have to be

Olivia Newton-John – even though she was the dark one and I was the blonde one. We used to practise in the school field.'

Victoria's love of pop music was not that surprising however, as her dad, Tony, had been a professional singer before beginning his current business. He was in a little-known Sixties band called The Sonics. Victoria would later say, 'Dad cut short his pop career to marry mum and so he's reliving what he wanted to do through me.'

The next stop for Victoria was the local secondary school, St Mary's High, in nearby Cheshunt. Here too she is recalled with affection by her teachers. 'She was very conscientious, very quiet,' says Marion Ellard, director of vocational studies at the school. 'Victoria didn't really stand out as an amazingly dynamic person. In fact, she was quite a joy to teach. She paid attention and worked hard.'

Even at this early stage, there was already a hint of the Posh Spice that Victoria was to become. 'She was one of a group of friends who were all very much the same sort – very nice young ladies. They were very image-conscious. They'd dress smartly and behave with maturity,' says Marion Ellard.

Head teacher Terry James tells the same story. 'She was such a pleasant and nicely-spoken young woman, always immaculately turned out in terms of uniform and always concerned about her work.'

But it was that care about her schoolwork and appearance which was beginning to attract unwelcome attention. While Mr James was unaware of bullying during Victoria's school years, he does remember that she stood out, not least because of her family background. 'They were pretty well off – and other children knew that,' he says.

Victoria herself has no doubts about why she fell prey to the bullies. Years later, in an interview with *Sugar* magazine, she explained: 'My parents had worked really hard and so were comfortably well off and people seemed to resent that. They'd brought me up the way that they thought was proper. I never used to swear or anything like that and so I was "uncool". It was "uncool" to come from a nice family, work hard and be polite.'

She claims: 'I never had lots of friends at senior school, not even in the beginning. You would never have called me a "popular" girl. If anything I was the least popular, and I hated it. What really used to get me is that I never really "asked" for trouble. You know how it is: some girls can be stuck up or think they're great or whatever. With me, I was just quiet.

'I know why they picked on me, though. It was because I used to work very hard at school. I was an outsider. I just wasn't like the other people at school. I didn't used to go smoking behind the bike sheds. When everyone else used to go out at night and hang out around the newsagent's, or wherever, I wouldn't. I had loads of hobbies and stuff that I'd do out of school. Anyway, even if I'd had the time, my mum would have never let me do that kind of thing.'

Among the things that got Victoria noticed most, however, was her dad's Rolls Royce. Emma Comolli remembers: 'She used to turn up in a really smart car while all the others went by bus. After school, her dad would wait for her in his gold-coloured Rolls Royce. It was quite a rough school, and nobody really had much money, so nobody liked this very much.'

Victoria also has vivid memories of the trip to school. 'The other kids used to travel in by bus, but because we didn't live that close, my dad used to drive us there . . . My dad has two cars: a van for his business deliveries and another car which happened to be a Rolls Royce.

'I remember Dad used to want to take us in the car and almost every day I'd go: "No, Dad! Please, please, take us in the van." I couldn't deal with the hassle I'd get when we arrived. There were days when I'd wish I came from a different family.'

But the bullies reserved their cruellest comments for the acne which affected Victoria during her teenage years. Emma Comolli says: 'Victoria had a really tough time. Not many people liked her. Her skin was terrible because she had really bad acne.' The gang which made her life a misery was nicknamed 'the Mafia' at the school, and Victoria was their favourite target, particularly after she told everyone that she was going to be famous one day. 'The others would turn on her and call her names,' says Emma. 'They used to throw Victoria's coat on the floor and trample on it, ripping it to bits. She certainly had a bad time.'

Victoria has not forgotten how she felt during that period. 'I remember I'd go to classes and be petrified. I'd usually get pushed around and sworn at, and then the girls who did it would say things like: "We're going to get you after school." Later on, they'd all be standing there waiting for me at the school gates, pushing me around.

'Those girls never actually beat me up, but that's irrelevant. It was the waiting for things to happen that was the torture. Sometimes mental bullying is worse than physical bullying. It's important that people realize that. For a while, I was a complete wreck. I would wake up worrying about who I was going to go out with at lunchtime and who I was going to sit with in class.'

By now the problem had become so great

that Victoria dreaded even going to school. 'I'd feel sick at the thought of school. I can't explain how horrible being bullied made me feel. It was pure hell. After holidays, I'd be nearly sick at the thought of going back.

'You know when, just before term starts, you go into C & A and Marks & Spencer, and all the signs are hanging up saying: "Back To School"? Just the sight of those signs used to make me physically sick. Looking back, I realize I didn't really turn to anybody for help. There were a few mates at school, but they weren't too supportive. You know how it is, friends at school won't necessarily stick up for you because the bullies are tougher and have more people with them.'

Victoria says that it was only when she grew older and made clear that the bullying was not affecting her that it began to wear off. She adds that the support of her close-knit family was also very important in helping her get through those difficult times.

'The only advice I could really give would be to get help. Don't be afraid to ask for it when you need it. The other thing to say is that you mustn't be depressed about being unpopular if you're just being yourself.'

There was one hobby above all which helped Victoria forget her troubles at school. As her mum, Jackie, recalls: 'Dancing was all Victoria ever wanted to do.' Since the age of eight she had been enrolled at the local Jason Theatre School, whose owner, Joy Spriggs, was immediately impressed by her new recruit.

She says, 'The very first time I saw her dance I knew Victoria was special. She performed for us in a wonderful costume covered in gold sequins. She had natural talent and you just had to watch her. She stayed with us until she was seventeen and won many awards with us. She lived, ate, slept and drank dancing.'

Victoria's first public performance was at the dance school, where she danced to a song which would turn out to have an appropriate title considering the stardom awaiting her: 'If My Friends Could See Me Now'. 'I just thought, this girl has got something,' Joy Spriggs remembers. 'She wasn't trained, but she finished by doing the splits. She danced instinctively.' Even when Victoria was not performing, she was an ever present at the school, watching and learning – and proving that she possessed another ability that would prove vital to her later becoming a Spice Girl. As Joy Spriggs puts it: 'She was always in the front row – she had an ability to get herself noticed.'

At this stage in her life, dancing still remained of far greater importance to Victoria than boys. Another friend from her teens, Sarah Buckle, says, 'We thought we were too old for school, and the boys there were all too young. We used to hang around with boys from a local private school.' Victoria did not have her first real boyfriend until she was sixteen. He was called Mark Wood, and for a while the relationship looked serious.

Sarah Buckle remembers that the couple became engaged, but they broke up before Victoria became successful with the Spice Girls.

Her next step was a three-year course at

the Laine Arts Theatre College, in Epsom, Surrey, England. After completing that, Victoria joined the cast of a small touring musical company in a production which ran for three months. Out of work for a short while, she finally joined a new pop group called Persuasion. Fellow member Steven Andrews, who recruited her, says, 'She walked into the room and looked great. She was a shy mummy's girl, but that was half the attraction. She wasn't a great singer but she had potential and I knew I had found the right girl. She was hungry for fame and willing to work hard.'

But she was not to be with them for long. The years of hard work which had made her the butt of the bullies' cruelty in her school-days were about to pay off. As she was later to say, 'At the end of the day, I was an under-dog who came through. All five of us in the end were the same, and that's what binds us together.'

For she had just spotted an advert looking for girls to join a new band – and her life was about to be changed for ever.

CHAPTER THREE

Sporty Spice – Mel C

Mel C's image is unmistakable. Often dressed in an England football shirt, Adidas tracksuit, and trainers, she is the tomboy of the Spice Girls, the one who hero-worships Liverpool Football Club, and actually plays for a women's soccer team.

She is seen as fit and tough too, back-flipping and karate-kicking on stage. So it comes as a surprise to learn that her schoolfriends remember Mel C as someone who was almost the complete opposite of the person she is known as now. What emerges is a picture of a girl whose greatest passion was for ballet, and who wanted to be a dancer rather than a singer. Everyone who does talk about her recalls her with affection and as a person who, in the words of one friend, 'was destined to be famous.'

Melanie Jayne Chisholm was born on 12 January 1974 in Whiston Hospital, Merseyside, England. At first she lived in nearby Rainhill but when she was aged seven her parents, Alan and Joan, split up. Her dad now works for a travel firm and he lives with his second wife in Leeds. Her mum eventually met another man, taxi driver Den O'Neill – who is Mel's stepdad – and they moved to the town of Widnes, and a small three-bedroomed terraced house where they still live. Soon afterwards, her half-brother Paul was born.

The person responsible as much as anyone for creating a love of performing in young Melanie was probably her mum. Although by day she is a secretary for a local council, Joan is better known around the pubs and clubs of Widnes as a singer in a band called T-Junction, which also includes husband

Den. She loves performing Tina Turner songs, and is said to have always dreamed of being famous herself. In her younger days she was in another band called Love Potion, who even released a couple of singles.

One of Mel's old schoolfriends, Zoe Curlett, who still lives in the area, has little doubt about the influence that mum, Joan, had on Mel. 'Her mum is with the band every weekend. She has a terrific voice, and it's obvious where Mel gets it from.'

Joan encouraged Mel to start going to ballet classes, which she attended every Saturday. It quickly became her favourite pastime, and when she wasn't doing that she was looking after the family's cats to which she was very close. Another of her friends from Fairfield County High School in Widnes, Mark Devany, says, 'She was ballet-mad and wasn't into football. She was a prefect, very quiet and always played the good girl. No one can believe that she's ended up as a Spice Girl.'

School also gave Mel the opportunity to appear on stage for the first time. She met her first serious boyfriend, Ian McKnight, while playing the part of his mother in a production of the musical *Blood Brothers*, and Ian's younger brother, Keith, also remembers her in the school's version of *The Wiz* (the modern musical based on *The Wizard of Oz*). Even so, Keith could never have believed what lay around the corner for Mel.

By the time that she reached the age of sixteen, Mel's hopes of becoming a dancer were given a tremendous boost. She won a place at the Doreen Bird Dance School in Sidcup, Kent, England. At her audition for the school she performed a piece from the musical in which she had first appeared at school – *Blood Brothers*.

The notes from that audition illustrate the impression that she made. They read: 'Mel has a nice appeal. She is strong with a flexible body. Her audition piece from *Blood Brothers* was very nice. She is very bright and has good potential. Should do well.' It was enough to win her the place at the school that she wanted.

Sue Passmore, the artistic director at the

dance school, has good memories of the girl who went on to become one of their most famous pupils. 'Melanie was very strong. She was a hard-working and single-minded pupil,' she says.

It is a view backed up by another teacher, musical director Pat Izen. 'Melanie didn't have a particularly good voice when she arrived. It was gutsy,' she recalls. 'But she had an excellent ear. She was a real individual. She always stuck out for what she wanted.'

Mel left the dance school at the age of eighteen with excellent grades. But, as she was about to find out the hard way, they did not guarantee that she would find work as a professional dancer. She spent most of the next two years unemployed, although she found work in a chip shop for a short while, and she struggled to get the break she needed. In the meantime she moved into a flat with a certain Melanie Brown.

'I had mixed success,' says Mel now. 'I got down to the last few auditions for *Cats* – but it wasn't meant to be.' In fact, she reached the shortlist of five candidates, but was forced to miss the final audition because she was suffering from tonsillitis.

At this point, Mel could easily have despaired in the South of England and given up hope of a dancing career, perhaps returning instead to her home and family in Merseyside. But before she even had the chance to consider such a prospect, that long awaited break turned up.

It might not have looked like much of a break at the time, and it wasn't the sort of dancing job for which she had trained. But it was about to turn Melanie Chisholm into a star.

CHAPTER FOUR

Baby Spice – Emma

As the youngest of the Spice Girls, Emma is the one the rest of the band feel needs looking after the most. But her cute appearance, with her hair in bunches, hides the fact that she has a longer experience of the show-business world than any of the other four girls.

Ever since she was a toddler, Emma has been performing either on stage or in front of a camera. As a child she was a model, dancer, and actress. It was in many ways the perfect preparation and upbringing for a future Spice Girl. It was as if her early life was simply a rehearsal for the day when she would eventually join the group.

Emma Lee Bunton was born on 21 January 1976 in Barnet, north London, England. Her parents – dad Trevor, a milkman, and mum Pauline – lived in a small third-floor flat in nearby Finchley. Four years later there was another addition to the Bunton household in the shape of Emma's younger brother, Paul, who is known as 'P.J.'

Her grandmother, Theresa Bunton, says it was clear very quickly that Emma was going to be an attention-grabber. 'We all said Emma would be someone special. She was a little dolly, the prettiest thing you have ever seen.'

While you might expect a doting granny to say exactly that, she was not alone in her opinion. At the age of only three, Emma won a beauty contest while the family was on holiday. As soon as they returned home, her mum Pauline wasted no time in enrolling her daughter at a children's modelling agency in north London.

Once again, she quickly made an impression. Agent Gill Peters recalls: 'Emma was a hit. She never stopped working and had that special something which we were always looking for – a sort of twinkle in the eye. She loved the camera.'

The cameras obviously liked Emma too. She was soon earning up to twenty pounds an hour modelling clothes in women's magazines and for the Mothercare catalogue. Between the ages of six and twelve, she spent many summers abroad modelling in holiday resorts such as Lanzarote and Corsica, and her mum Pauline saved the money that Emma earned to help pay for drama school fees later. She also appeared in television commercials, starring as the Milky Bar kid's girlfriend in one, while in another her face smiled out from boxes of Persil washing powder.

Another of the young girls who modelled in the Mothercare catalogue, Crystal Power, says Emma was perfect for the job and kind to the other girls who worked with her. 'She was very professional,' says Crystal. 'If the little ones cried, Emma gave them a hug and told them everything would be all right.'

Emma was only four years old when she began attending a dance school near her home in Finchley. Her ex-instructor Sheryl Adrian regarded the little blonde girl as her star pupil. 'She was a skinny little stick who took jazz, ballet and tap dancing. Her first solo on stage was as a moonbeam in the school show, dressed in a peach tutu. Then she was a tap-dancing bear cub.

'I will never forget how well she fitted in, even with children two years older. I remember one line-up when she picked up a particularly complicated routine right away.' Sheryl adds: 'I knew she wanted to do something with music. She was extremely good at everything so I knew that she would go far.'

Her former head teacher at the local St Theresa's Roman Catholic Primary School, Dennis Carey, also had a feeling that his pupil might make a career out of her favourite hobbies. 'She was always a happy child,' recalls Mr Carey, who still keeps in touch with Emma today. 'She loved singing, dancing and drama, and was very good at them all. She always had a smile on her face.'

Joining the Sylvia Young Theatre School in London was a turning point for Emma. She passed the audition at the age of ten to win a place at the school which has a reputation for turning out future stars.

Among Emma's fellow pupils in the dance class, for instance, were television presenter Dani Behr, Daniella Westbrook, who would later go on to play Sam Butcher in *EastEnders*, and another actress Samantha Janus. But one of her closest friends was Denise Van Outen, who is now one of the presenters of Channel 4's *The Big Breakfast*.

'Emma was a great singer and lovely as a person,' says Denise now. 'Everyone liked her, and even then she wore her hair in bunches.' Denise even reveals that the two of them sometimes shared boyfriends. 'Emma and I were the two blondes at school. That made us quite popular with the boys. We'd meet in the toilets at break-time and talk about the boys we'd kissed. Quite often you'd find that you had been kissing the same ones.'

Denise adds, 'Girls outnumbered boys at

our school, which is probably where Emma got all that Girl Power from.' She was delighted to meet Emma again recently and discover that she hadn't changed. 'It was still the Emma I used to go to the chip shop with at lunchtime, and eat chocolate with on the way home from school.'

Emma has no doubts that the Sylvia Young Theatre School helped her to achieve future success. 'I loved dancing and singing when I was young and always wanted to be an actress or a pop star,' she says. 'The school was very good for me because it gave me the opportunity to achieve some of my ambitions.'

However, sending her to the school cost Emma's parents a great deal of money. Her grandmother recalls: 'It cost thousands of pounds to send her and they sometimes didn't have a penny to rub together. Pauline wasn't working so Trevor had to do three milk rounds a day as well as window cleaning and minicabbing. When she first started out as an actress, Trevor would rather go without food on the table than see her go without.'

By the time that brother P.J. was nine years old, the two of them were both auditioning for roles in soap operas, stage plays and radio shows. Emma appeared in programmes on British television, as well as winning a part in the stage musical, *Dick Whittington*. Her biggest role was as a member of an all-girl gang in *EastEnders* – a show to which she would later attempt to return.

At the age of twelve, Emma had also started attending karate classes at a church hall near her home, and got on particularly well with the teacher – which was not surprising really, as it was her mum, Pauline. She is now a blue belt, the fifth of nine grades in the sport.

'I trained to teach karate ... then Emma decided to do it, mainly to keep fit and in case she got into any trouble,' says Pauline, who is a black belt at the sport – the highest grade. 'She trained two or three times a week and was very good at it. She never missed a class.'

Emma's dreams of becoming a dancer suffered something of a blow when she suffered a back injury at the age of fourteen. Worse was to follow two years later when her mum and dad separated after fifteen years of marriage. Her dad moved out, and now lives in Whetstone only a couple of miles from the flat where Emma was born, lodging in a flat above a fast-food restaurant, while her mum lives with Emma and P.J. in Essex, England.

But the setbacks only seemed to make Emma more determined to be successful. She went to Barnet College in north London to study drama, and to win roles in television series. Her efforts looked like being rewarded when she was offered the chance to audition for a new part in *EastEnders*. It wasn't just a bit-part either. The producers of the show were looking for someone who would play an important character in Albert Square.

Unfortunately for Emma, she was pipped to the post by Patsy Palmer for the role of Bianca in the soap. It seemed that her hopes of appearing in front of millions of people had been dashed. But she need not have worried. Her next audition was just around the corner, and it would bring her the sort of fame which even a top show like *EastEnders* could never match.

SCARY SPICE – MEL B

CHAPTER FIVE
Scary Spice – Mel B

It's easy to see why Mel B is known as the
scary one out of the Spice Girls. She often
wears army boots and combat trousers,
she is loud, brash, and when she does start
talking you also notice that she has a pierced
tongue. Along with Geri, she is the member of
the band most likely to speak her mind.

Her mum, Andrea, is more aware than
most of Mel's habit of saying what she thinks.
For at one time she was worried that it would
be her daughter's downfall, particularly after
teachers warned her that Mel's big mouth
would not help her get on in the outside
world once she left school.

But the feisty girl, who also had to cope with prejudice in her early years because she is the child of a white mother and black father, has surprised everyone who doubted her. Like the rest of the Spice Girls, it soon becomes clear that Mel's sheer determination to be famous was the key to her ultimate success.

Melanie Janine Brown was born on 29 May 1975 in Leeds, England. Her mum Andrea, is a cleaner at the city's C&A department store, and dad, Martin, was a shift worker at a local engineering company. Despite having one of the best-known daughters in Britain, Martin doesn't have a car and still travelled to work each day on his bicycle until he recently lost his job. He and Andrea live in the modest, red-brick semi-detached house in the Burley area of Leeds where Mel grew up, keeping rabbits in the back garden. Mel's younger sister Danielle lives with them, and works as a shop assistant.

From the earliest years of her life, Mel's parents were aware that their eldest daughter wanted to be involved in acting, dancing, or singing. Mum, Andrea, recalls: 'Mel has loved performing since she was little. Everybody knew that she wanted to be famous.'

Her parents encouraged Mel's dreams. She started taking ballet and acting lessons. But it quickly became evident that this was not going to be enough. The solution was the Intake High School in nearby Bramley, West Yorkshire, England, the only school in the area offering a performing arts course. Mel applied – and was accepted.

Her classmates at the new school included other girls who would one day become famous. One was Angela Griffin, best known today as Fiona Middleton, the hairdresser in *Coronation Street* – and someone who would cross Mel's path again after both had left Intake High School. But her closest friend was Rebecca Callard.

Rebecca is now an actress, and has appeared in the much-loved children's series, *The Borrowers*, on BBC1 as well as a recent television drama series, *The Grand*, set in a hotel during the 1920s. Rebecca's mum is also a familiar face on television screens, for she is Bev Callard, who plays Liz McDonald in *Coronation Street*. Bev says: 'Mel and Rebecca are still firm friends. Mel was a lovely bubbly girl and she and Rebecca just hit it off. Mel hasn't changed at all.'

Rebecca, now in her early twenties, easily recalls the moment that she and Mel met. 'When I first saw her at school, I thought: "Who is that beautiful girl? She is amazing." We started talking and have been friends ever since.' The two of them once bought each other eyeshadow, and Rebecca still has the one Mel bought for her, which she keeps as a cherished possession. 'She's my oldest and dearest friend. I was always in complete awe of her as a youngster,' she says.

The two girls still get together occasionally for a night out, but Rebecca admits that it is easier for her than it is for Mel. 'Our jobs are so very different. She's a household name and gets recognized everywhere she goes, whereas at least I can change out of the part I'm playing.'

When Rebecca does get spotted in the street it is often because people confuse her for another of Mel's good friends because of her red hair. 'I do get recognized, but quite a lot of people think I'm Geri from the Spice Girls,' says Rebecca. 'It drives me nuts especially as they have become so popular. I have been in changing rooms looking at clothes and people have followed me in thinking I'm Geri.

'Melanie and I don't see each other very often these days because she is so busy. But we speak to each other a lot on the phone. Although I am delighted about her success, I do find it upsetting because I miss her company,' says Rebecca.

But Rebecca claims that what gives her the greatest satisfaction about the success that both she and Mel have enjoyed is that no one at school expected them to do particularly well. 'People thought we'd never amount to much and that there was no hope for us. They just thought we were dizzy girls, because neither of us were good at maths and science.'

Mel's mum, Andrea, also knew of the concern that some teachers had for Mel's future.

'I always knew she couldn't do a nine-to-five job and I feared her personality might be her downfall. Even her teachers once told me she would never go anywhere because of her mouth. I thought they might be right. But I'm so proud of her now.'

Her former teacher, David Robbins, head of performing arts at Intake High School, remembers Mel fondly. 'She loved being on stage and playing to an audience. I knew then that she was going to make it big.' Mel's performance in a production of *Jesus Christ Superstar* particularly stands out in his memory. 'She didn't have a star acting part, but I chose her to perform a major song. It was a gospel song and she was perfect for it because she has a lovely deep, strong voice.'

While her upbringing was a happy one, there were times when Mel experienced problems because of her mixed-race background. Rebecca Callard says they have suffered name-calling in the past while out together, but the incident which sticks with Mel herself concerned her parents. One night, while she was still a child, her mother and father were banned entry to a local club in Leeds. The reason, Mel says, was because her father is black.

'The place refused us family membership – I think because of my mixed race parents. That's so small-minded,' she says. She remembers the promise that she made herself at the time: 'The first thing I'll do when I get rich is buy that club.'

Mel left Intake High School at the age of sixteen, and went from there to the Leeds College of Music to study singing. At the same time, she signed up for a part-time two-year course at the Northern School of Contemporary Dance. But, as a student, she was always struggling to make ends meet so, to earn a little money, she danced at a Leeds night club called The Yell.

Her former boss at the club, Lisa Adamczyk, says that Mel was a different person to the outspoken girl that her mother and friends remember from her schooldays, not to mention the character she has become in the Spice Girls. 'It's quite funny looking at her now because in the old days she wouldn't say boo to a goose. Sure, she was a great mover and a very professional dancer. But it was all just an act. When she came off stage she'd throw on an old sweatshirt and jogging pants, pick up her bag and her wages, and go home.

'The other dancers used to join the staff and go out clubbing or for a meal, but never Mel. She was a sweet, quiet girl who wanted to get on. I'm really pleased she has. She's a perfect example of what can be done if you work hard enough,' says Lisa. She adds: 'One of Mel's routines at The Yell club was to the song "The Only Way Is Up". What a hell of a prophecy that turned out to be.'

Mel first got her face in the newspapers when she was only seventeen, but it was hardly on the same scale as the ceaseless national press coverage that she and the rest of the Spice Girls now receive. Instead, she was named the winner in a local beauty contest, Miss Leeds Weekly News 1992. The prizes included the use of a Renault Clio car for one year, a weekend for two at Disneyland in Paris, and a modelling course. She said at the time: 'I can't believe it. It's the first time I've been in for a contest like this. I'm amazed I even got this far.'

Among those delighted by this triumph was Mel's first serious boyfriend. Stephen Mullrain was a football player with the local team, Leeds United, and regarded as a very promising prospect. But, sadly, his career was cut short by a head injury that same year, when he was only eighteen. Friends say that Mel and Stephen were inseparable for a while. But the lure of London was pulling Mel away, and the couple eventually parted.

Mel had decided to move down to the capital after being accepted by the trainee skating school which taught future cast members of the hugely successful Andrew Lloyd Webber musical on wheels, *Starlight Express*. She also managed to get on television, as one of a group of dancers performing with a country and western music group in a television comedy called *September Song*. One of her fellow dancers was Tracy Shaw, who would later also achieve stardom as hairdresser Maxine in *Coronation Street*.

'You gotta get with my friends' –
the girls together

Doing their bit for Comic Relief

It's all under control –
at the launch of Channel 5

Liverpool's greatest fan –
Mel C

Smouldering Victoria –
the posh Spice

Not too old for teddy bears –
baby Emma

Look out! –
it's scary Mel B

Pop's cheekiest smile –
Geri

John Dean, one of the singers in the country and western group, says: 'Mel was a brilliant laugh, though her voice arrived in the room about ten minutes before she did!'

Soon after going to London, Mel moved into a flat with another girl who was like her – a dancer who spent much of her day going to one audition after another, looking for the job that might get her noticed. The other girl's name was Melanie Chisholm.

Before long, both girls would be attending an audition which would get them noticed beyond their wildest dreams.

CHAPTER SIX
Ginger Spice – Geri

Geri is the natural leader of the Spice Girls. The reason is not simply because she is the oldest of the five girls, but because of the sheer strength of her character. Even more than Mel B, Geri is the one who will always make herself heard.

Her lively personality and determination to grab the headlines at every opportunity probably date back to a childhood which was very different to that of Victoria, for instance. While Geri sought the chance to go to the same dancing and singing classes as the rest of the girls attended when they were young, she was prevented from doing so because her parents were not that well off. But what Geri might have lacked once in money, she more than made up for in resourcefulness and bare-faced cheek.

That ability to get herself noticed has made Geri probably the most high profile of the Spice Girls, and the one who best represents what the band is all about.

Geraldine Estelle Halliwell was born in Watford, Hertfordshire, England, on 6 August 1972. Her mother, Anna, is Spanish, but she left her home country as an eighteen-year-old more than thirty years ago to find work in England. It was here that she met motor-car dealer, Liverpool-born Laurence Halliwell, who had already been married once and had two children – Geri's half-brother Paul, and her half-sister Karen, who now acts as Geri's personal assistant and dress designer.

Laurence and Anna married and settled in Watford where they had three children – Max, born in 1967, Natalie, born in 1969, and finally Geri, who arrived three years later. However, her parents' marriage was not destined to last.

When Geri was only ten years old, they split up and her father moved out.

Her brother Max says that Geri's desire to be a performer was not immediately obvious. 'As a toddler she wasn't that much different to the rest of us, but eventually it became evident that Geri would be well suited to show business. At school she was quiet and got on with her work, but at home she would always be singing at the top of her voice and dancing. She had one favourite song which ran, "I wannabe a night club queen, the most exciting you've ever seen."'

Her energy at school meanwhile was channelled into netball. She was captain of the team at the Walter de Merton Junior School in Watford. Geri's friend, Scott Smith, who was twelve years old at the time, remembers walking her home from netball practice holding her hand. 'She was cute, but very skinny,' says Scott now. 'I think she had a crush on me but I didn't want to go out with her and I never kissed her.'

Many summers and Christmas holidays were spent at the flat of her mum's sister,

Geri's favourite aunt – Maria Hidalgo Pueyo – in the northern Spanish town of Huesca, nestling in the foothills of the Pyrenees. Geri would often be taught Spanish in the afternoon, and also told of her family's aristocratic past, for she is a direct descendant of Prince Pedro Hidalgo of Cordoba, a legendary figure from six hundred years ago, who was once said to have killed ten of his opponents in battle at one go. The family would also go trekking in the surrounding hills and Geri learned to ski at the nearby resort of Formigal.

Sometimes the children would even be taken to watch the bullfighting, but it was not one of Geri's favourite pastimes. 'Geri used to cry when the bull was killed,' says her Aunt Maria. 'She always wanted us to take it home, to save it.'

Her Aunt Maria thinks that Geri's personality takes after hers. 'Inside Geri is just like me – a rebel who needs a firm hand,' she claims. 'We are both explosive and impulsive and we rowed from the moment that she was big enough to sit on my knee. She is like a pineapple – soft and sweet on the inside but with a tough exterior for the outside world.'

By the time that Geri reached her teens, she had moved to Watford Girls' School where she was a popular pupil who always told her classmates that she wanted to be a model. The problem, however, was that at that stage she was rather small and thin, something for which she was teased.

Geri left school at the age of sixteen, with one A level pass in English Literature. While she was unsure exactly what she wanted to do, she already knew that it had to be something in show business. But for the moment, she had to take a number of odd jobs to earn a living. Besides baby-sitting neighbours' children, she spent time working in a video rental store, trying her hand as a hairdresser, and serving in bars and shops. Geri would save money so that she could record tapes of herself singing and then send them to record companies.

She was still living with her mum, Anna, who works as a cleaner in the Harlequin Centre, a shopping mall in Watford. Even though her daughter is now rich and famous,

Anna still prefers to sweep floors, pick up litter and empty bins at the Centre, saying, 'Geri makes a lot of money and wanted me to give up my cleaning job. But I like it too much. I was doing it before Geri became famous so why should I give it up?'

Geri's next move was to decide to travel in search of her fortune. At one stage she even worked as a game-show hostess on a television station in Turkey. Then, on the Spanish island of Majorca, she tried her hand as a dancer and a model. Des Mitchell, a disc jockey at the club in Majorca where she danced for customers, recalls: 'She worked very hard at her dancing. Everyone knew she wanted to be famous. This was the first stepping stone.'

Eventually, Geri returned to Watford but her single-minded pursuit of fame remained constant. For two hours every day she worked with local sports coach Ray McKenna to get herself fit and in shape. 'I couldn't believe how determined she was,' he says. 'She said: "I'm going to be famous and I want my body to be perfect."

'At six forty-five every morning we ran for forty-five minutes. It was often dark, cold and raining, but Geri would never complain. She was more dedicated than anyone I know. She was so fit and had amazing stamina.' Not satisfied with just this training programme, Geri also started her own aerobics class, putting other people through their paces.

While she lived with her mum, Geri remained in close contact with her dad, Laurence. By this stage he had retired from his job, but he was always urging Geri to go after the career of her dreams. 'If you want it enough, it will be yours,' he used to tell her. Geri's brother Max reveals that their father also drove her to many of her auditions.

Sadly for Geri, her father was not around to help her much longer. He died at the age of seventy-one in November 1993, a loss which really upset his youngest daughter. It is one of her biggest regrets that her father did not live to see her become famous. For it was only a few months after his death that Geri was to turn up at the audition for which she had spent her whole life preparing.

CHAPTER SEVEN
Wannabes

The advert was placed in *The Stage* – the newspaper for all the performing arts – and it was brief and direct. It read:

'R.U. 18–23 with the ability to sing/dance? R.U. streetwise, outgoing, ambitious and dedicated?

Heart Management Ltd are a widely-successful music industry management con-sortium, currently forming a choreographed, singing/dancing, all-female pop act for a record recording deal.'

The advert went on to ask for applicants to send in photographs of themselves and demo tapes of how they sounded if they possessed them, and provided an address to which to write. It was from this advert that the Spice Girls were eventually created.

Heart Management, the company mentioned in the advert, belonged to two men – Chris Herbert and his father, Bob. They had already been involved in pop music, having spotted the huge teeny-bop success of the late-Eighties group, Bros.

Their idea this time was to form an all-girl band to rival the enormously successful all-boy creations of the time, such as Take That and East 17. The Herberts thought that the new group would be made up of five very different characters, but who were all strong-willed and tough-talking. The two men joined forces with a London businessman called Chick Murphy, who provided money for the Herberts' latest project.

In answer to the advert in *The Stage*, more than 400 hopeful girls turned up at the Dreamworks studio just off London's Oxford

Street on 4 March 1994. They were given a short space of time in which to perform then given marks out of ten, not just for their singing, but also based on such factors as their dancing, their looks and their personalities. After these first auditions, a shortlist of eight candidates emerged. It included Victoria Adams, Melanie Chisholm and Melanie Brown. Geri Halliwell and Emma Bunton would not enter the picture until somewhat later.

As a video of their auditions (which has since been released) illustrates, Mel C appeared among the most confident of those chosen. Drawing on her already considerable experience of attending many similar auditions, she performed 'I'm So Excited', an Eighties' hit for the American girl band, The Pointer Sisters. At the end of her song, she cheekily nodded at the judges as she left the stage. She was picked.

Mel B looked rather more nervous as she sang her version of Whitney Houston's 'The Greatest Love of All', while Victoria, who was already in a band, impressed those watching as someone who was an all-rounder – able to sing and dance. Both of them were also told that they were in. But the girl who scored the highest marks was a drama student called Michelle Stephenson. Her singing voice was excellent, and her performance of 'Don't Be A Stranger', the song which was a hit for Dina Carroll, even won a round of applause from the watching judges. The new band now had four members.

But the Herberts still wanted one more girl. At this point, Chris Herbert received a telephone call from a desperate-sounding Geri Halliwell. She explained that she had been forced to miss the first auditions because of a modelling job, and pleaded for an opportunity to prove herself. She was given that chance the following month on 29 April 1994, and her personality quickly won over those watching. Now there were five.

The next part of the plan was to coach the new group in how to sing and perform together. The first time that all five of them met was on 7 June 1994 at the Trinity Studios in Woking, Surrey, England run by Ian Lee.

He recalls: 'They all had talent, but were not used to working together.' He adds: 'But they had one thing in common and that was blind ambition.'

After one week of practising at the studios and staying in a local bed and breakfast, the girls were told that they had a fortnight to decide whether or not they were sure that this was what they wanted to do. All five of them made it plain that they were determined to continue. From that point onwards, the really hard work began.

The management now moved the group to live together in Maidenhead, Berkshire, England. In a modern, red-brick semi-detached house in Boyn Hill Road, the girls would at last get to know each other, forming the bonds between them which are evident today, as they spent their days in the studio, and their evenings in the house together. They were allowed pocket money, and had all their bills and rent paid. This was to be their life for the next nine months.

A voice trainer was brought in to help the girls' singing voices. Pepi Lemer, who had by coincidence taught a young Emma Bunton in singing classes while she was at theatre school, worked with the would-be band for a four-hour session, twice a week, through-out the nine months at Maidenhead. 'There were quite a few times when I really had to gee them up. They really didn't want to have to go through all this, it was hard work,' said Pepi later. 'One might have a headache, the other would start crying, another would run out of the room and the remainder would start arguing.'

Remembering all the time that he spent with the group in his recording studios, Ian Lee tells a similar story. He says that the different characters of the band members now started to emerge most clearly – and that two in particular soon took charge.

'Geri and Melanie Brown were instantly singled out as the leaders. They always had an opinion and they both wanted to be in the driving seat. They used to fight like cat and dog,' claims Ian. 'Geri would stand there with her arms by her sides and her fists clenched as Mel would have a go at her for singing out of tune. Mel Chisholm would always act the peacemaker and the other girls would just watch in stunned silence.'

According to Ian Lee, Geri was aware that her singing and dancing ability needed improvement, and worked harder than most to achieve it. 'She'd spend hours on her own perfecting her singing or working on her dance steps. She was determined to succeed,' he says. 'She kept saying: "Time's running out. This is my last chance and I'm going to make it." She was a tough nut.'

Pepi Lemer was also struck by Geri's single-mindedness. 'Initially, Geri didn't like me,' she says. 'I had written notes on all of them after hearing them sing and she saw what I had written by her name – "out of tune". She burst into tears. I took her aside and told her quite firmly that she had to be professional. But I grew to admire her,' Pepi adds. 'What she may have lacked in raw talent, she made up for in drive and ambition. She was so hungry for fame.'

Geri was not the only one. Mark Brown-smith, who was then Mel B's boyfriend, says that the entire band was convinced of their destiny. 'The girls were always saying they were going to become famous. They told us: "Take That are finished – this time next year, we'll be them."'

After they had been together for a few months in Maidenhead, it became apparent, however, that Michelle Stephenson was not fitting in. 'She wasn't like the rest of the girls,' says Ian Lee. 'She was quite reserved and wouldn't always agree to do the things the rest of them wanted. It was obvious that something was going to have to be done.'

But before anything was done, Michelle heard some devastating news – her mother, Penny, was seriously ill. Her mother says now: 'It was a very difficult time for Michelle. I was being treated for breast cancer and it was a time when she wanted to be with me. Later she had to make a decision whether to stay with the group or to go back to finish her studies.

'She thought about it long and hard but eventually decided to go back to college. The Spice Girls thing came at the wrong time in her life, although she doesn't regret her decision at all. She's pleased that the girls are doing so well, but she knew in her heart that it wasn't for her.'

Voice trainer Pepi Lemer suggested a possible replacement – an eighteen-year-old girl who was then at college in central London, and who had been a pupil of hers in the past. Abigail Kis went along for an audition at which she sang a soul ballad, and two days later was contacted with the news that she had been successful. The management were impressed not just with her voice, but because they thought her dark complexion and eyes were the sort of exotic look that the band needed. But Abigail, who is half-Hungarian, did not share their certainty.

She explains now: 'It was a huge gamble. I had a place at Middlesex University to do an honours degree in performing arts and I was not sure if I should give it up. Also, it all sounded such hard work, and I didn't know if I wanted to commit to it.' What concerned Abigail most however was the prospect of having to move into the house in

Maidenhead with the rest of the girls. 'I was really young and I did not want to be uprooted. I had been going out with my boy-friend for three-and-a-half years and I knew our relationship would suffer.'

So Abigail turned down the offer – something that she now admits she regrets, especially considering that she eventually split up with her boyfriend anyway. 'Every time I see them I think: "It could have been me." I would have loved to have been that famous.' Now a trainee aerobics teacher, Abigail first realized that the band she nearly joined had hit the big time when she saw them early on in their career on breakfast television. 'When I heard them say that they were all living together, everything fell into place.'

The management again turned to Pepi Lemer, who recalled another of her former pupils – Emma Bunton. Ian Lee says that it was obvious immediately that she would settle in. 'She was far more suited to the rest of the girls, although she would go on about how much she missed her mum,' he remembers. 'She and Victoria were real family girls and always went home at weekends.'

While the final line-up was the one that we now know, the band was not at that time called the Spice Girls. For their first few months together, they were known as Touch, and there are differing stories about how they came up with the name that would soon become famous throughout the world.

Ian Lee explains one version. 'They got their name from Tim Hawes who co-wrote a song with them and titled it "Sugar and Spice". They were sitting around afterwards and he said: "There's your name. It's perfect because you're a spicy bunch." They loved it.'

But pensioner Mabel Brobyn, who lived next door to the girls during their stay in Boyn Hill Road, Maidenhead, believes that the real answer is linked to her pet Lakeland Terrier dog called Spice. 'Occasionally the girls came over to ask my husband for help,' she says. 'One time, they had locked themselves out and he lent them a ladder. Spice was always around and we'd constantly be calling out his name. I'm sure that's where they got it.'

Whatever the real story, there was no doubt that the girls were growing in self-belief all the time. 'You could see that they were going to make it,' says Ian Lee. 'They started to act like real pop stars.'

With no guarantee that the band would be successful, however, it was difficult for the girls to turn down other opportunities which came along. Mel B auditioned for the role of Fiona, who runs the hairdressing salon in *Coronation Street*. But she was pipped to the post by Angela Griffin who had been at the same school as her a few years previously. Geri, meanwhile, was offered the chance to present a children's show on a cable television channel. Her brother Max recalls: 'She could accept a very tempting job offer with guaranteed money, or ride her luck with the band. The chances of the band hitting the big time were pretty slim, but I don't think she hesitated.'

In January 1995, the band performed five songs (including one called, appropriately,

'We're Gonna Make It Happen') at a studio in Earl's Court, London – only a short distance from the arena where two years later they would collect their Brit Awards. On this occasion, however, they were trying to attract the attention of the record industry bosses, who had already heard rumours about this promising all-girl band. Many of the big recording labels sent along scouts to see and hear what was on offer.

Afterwards, the girls were filmed talking about their dreams and hopes. Victoria, her hair much longer than the bob that she now wears, can be seen saying: 'I really want this to succeed. It is something I have always wanted to do. We are all working really, really hard. We are all ambitious, which is good. We want to go in *Smash Hits* and on *Top of the Pops*.' Elsewhere on the video, Emma says, 'We want to make it big. I think we are all great and we can do it if we work hard.'

With interest in the girls increasing all the time, they finally parted company from Chris and Bob Herbert, and gained a new manager,

Simon Fuller, whose previous clients had included singer Annie Lennox. After considering the various offers, he signed the Spice Girls to the Virgin record label. Just as importantly, he introduced them to Eliot C. Kennedy, a song-writer who worked with Gary Barlow of Take That. Simon Fuller's job now was to ensure that the whole country knew about the group, so that people would then buy their records.

But while their careers were just starting to show signs of taking off, the girls still had a far tougher critic to convince that they were going to be famous – Mel B's mum, Andrea – and it needed one of their best performances to persuade her. She later recalled: 'I used to say to Mel that she should leave the group because they were broke. All the band had job offers, including Mel, but they turned them down to stick together.

'One day they all just stood in my living room and sang. There was no microphone or backing music. We were really shocked how good they were. We had never really heard them before. From that day on, I changed my attitude. I have encouraged her ever since.'

The girls came up with all sorts of publicity stunts to get themselves noticed and remembered. On one such occasion, they performed a very early public rendition of 'Wannabe' at Kempton Park racecourse, at one point climbing on top of the bronze statue of the Grand-National-winning horse, Red Rum, to the surprise and amusement of the gathered music industry spectators. It had the desired effect, catching the eye of Vincent Monsey, the man in charge of the cable television pop channel, *The Box*.

'When I saw the Spice Girls on top of Red Rum, their personalities came right through and I knew they would do something big,' he says. As a result, *The Box* started showing the video of 'Wannabe' – again and again. In fact, the channel played the video seventy times a week – an honour only normally granted to songs which have reached number one in the charts.

But, of course, that is precisely where 'Wannabe' was going.

CHAPTER EIGHT
Girl Power

There was something about the all-girl band Ralph Barber was watching on television at his home in Oldham, Lancashire, England, that made him look twice. He knew that a couple of them were familiar to him, but at first he could not put his finger on where he had seen them before. Then suddenly it came to him.

Nearly two years previously, Ralph and his wife had flown to the Mediterranean island of Gran Canaria to spend Christmas there. Staying in the same apartment block, taking a break from practice with their then unknown band, were Mel B and Geri. With a jolt he realized that it was them he was now watching on TV.

'My wife and I met the girls on the first day of the holiday and they were great fun,' Ralph recalls. 'They said they were in a band but hadn't had any success. I didn't believe them – so when I saw them on *Top of the Pops* I was completely shocked.'

Ralph, like millions of others, first became aware of the Spice Girls in July 1996, as 'Wannabe' started getting airplay on dozens of radio stations, while the video for the single appeared on British television's *Top of the Pops* and *The Chart Show*.

Their timing was perfect. Five months previously, Take That had gone their separate ways, leaving a gap in the market. Most people assumed that the band's main songwriter, Gary Barlow, would continue where Take That had left off, and he was the first to release a solo single, 'Forever Love', which went straight to number one. His ex-colleagues Robbie Williams and Mark Owen were also known to have recorded songs which were soon to come out.

But all of them were to be completely over-
whelmed by the Spice Girls. 'Wannabe'
entered the UK charts at number three on
14 July, the same week that Barlow was at
number one. And the following week, the
girls had replaced him at the top. In a very
short space of time, 'Wannabe' had established itself as the summer's catchiest hit, and
the lines 'I'll tell you what I want, what I
really, really want' and 'zigazig ha' were on
everyone's lips. The band had also become
the first British girl group to go to number
one with their first single.

The girls themselves were naturally
delighted to hear the news, which reached
them while they were touring in Japan.
'Going to number one hasn't sunk in for us
yet,' said Mel C. 'We've been working so
hard for the last two years. It's a great compli-
ment to be compared to Take That, because
they were so successful for such a long time.
But we are different.'

For Emma, the sudden stardom rep-
resented everything she had ever worked for
and wanted. 'I'd always dreamed of fame

and a career in pop or showbiz, so to have a taste of it at my age is a fantasy come true,' she said. 'All my life I have wanted to be successful, so I am prepared to work hard for my living. We aim to conquer the world, have a good time doing it and – most of all – spice things up a bit!'

In the ever-growing number of newspaper articles about the band, as well as their television appearances, the image of the Spice Girls was becoming firmly established. The public quickly learned that Geri was strong and independent, someone who 'lived on the edge'. Mel B was presented as wild and loud-mouthed, while Mel C was the one who wore tracksuits, talked about football a lot and worked out at the gym. Emma, the baby of the group, was described by friends as 'a Top Shop girl with her blonde hair and pink clothes. She drives a jeep and looks like Barbie.' Victoria, meanwhile, was 'the lady' of the group, it was revealed, who liked designer-label clothes and dark glasses.

The girls had no doubts about the identity they wanted to project. 'It's more than just another girl group,' Victoria insisted. 'Women have to shout louder than men to be heard and our music is great because it gives us an extremely loud voice. Our aim is to be an inspiration to other girls.' Emma agreed. 'Boys love us and that's great, but we're definitely out to appeal more to the girls,' she said.

Geri had another view about why Girl Power, as their appeal had already become known, was taking Britain by storm and winning so many girl fans. 'We're not too pretty so that we offend them,' she claimed. 'We're just like them, we want them to join our club.'

The band's recording company, Virgin, was also certain that a big change was taking place in British pop music. 'Girl Power is seeing off the boy bands,' said a spokesman. He added: 'The attraction for boy fans is obvious, because they are five very pretty girls with a lot to say for themselves. But a lot of young girls bought "Wannabe" as well, because at last they have role models who aren't middle-aged and singing about love – they are just out to have a good time.'

At this stage, however, most critics were inclined to regard the Spice Girls as a flash in the pan, despite the huge sales that 'Wannabe' was continuing to pile up each week. Within the first few weeks alone of its release, the song had sold more than 700,000 copies – an astonishing figure in such a short time.

'We're as shocked as everyone else by the success of "Wannabe",' said Victoria. 'It doesn't put us under any pressure to follow it up, though. If it's the only number one we ever have, at least it proves what we're capable of. It's brilliant because it was the public who put it there so it shows they enjoy what we do.' But Victoria was swift to point out that the band were taking nothing for granted. 'It's only one tiny step for us as a band. We've already recorded an album which we're incredibly proud of and that's what we're really anxious for people to get into.' She would soon discover that the girls had no worry on that score.

Throughout the summer of 1996, 'Wannabe' dominated the charts. It was at number one for seven weeks, and prevented other acts from reaching that top spot who would once have been considered certain to do so, including Robbie Williams with his first solo single, and even Michael Jackson. The Spice Girls' newly-established fan club could hardly cope with the number of people clamouring to join. By the end of the summer, its membership was 100,000 – and rising by 10,000 every week.

Besides eventually selling more than one-and-a-quarter-million copies in Britain, 'Wannabe' topped the charts in twenty-eight countries. As we shall later see, nowhere did it have a greater impact than the most important music market of all – America. For now, however, everyone was waiting to see what the Spice Girls would do to follow up their first single.

The answer was 'Say You'll Be There'. It was a complete change of pace from 'Wannabe''s boundless energy, a gentler and more romantic song. But it had exactly the same impact on the charts as its predecessor. Weeks before its official release, hundreds of thousands of orders were placed for 'Say You'll Be There'. So it was absolutely no surprise when that too went in to the UK charts at number one. Now everyone had heard of the Spice Girls. While signing copies of her new book at a store in Birmingham, even the Duchess of York revealed that she and her two daughters, the Princesses Beatrice and Eugenie, sang along in the car to the band's hits.

Meanwhile, the girls confirmed their outrageous reputation at every opportunity. It was reported that security guards had been called in at a BBC Radio 1 Roadshow in Birmingham, England during the summer, to keep watch on the dressing rooms of boy bands which the Spice Girls had threatened to trash. One un-named member of such a band was quoted as saying: 'When there are five of them together I get so scared I actually start to shake.' True or not, it certainly bolstered the girls' image.

There were other boys, however, who the band were very keen to meet. The girls revealed that their number-one hunk who they would most like to date was actor George Clooney, star of the television medical drama *ER* and the latest *Batman* movie. Next most popular was Liverpool footballer Jamie Redknapp, and also in the Spice Girls' top-ten favourite men were actors Denzil Washington, Bruce Willis, Brad Pitt, and *EastEnders* star Paul Nicholls who plays Joe Wicks.

But while they talked about celebrities, the girls tended to go out with boys who were far removed from the glamorous world in which they now moved. Emma's boyfriend was revealed to be Mark Verquese, a twenty-one-year-old who worked in a dental surgery. He lived not far from her family home in north London, and she later took him on holiday with her mother and brother to the Caribbean island of Barbados, though they have since parted. 'I've always gone for real blokes … I'm not into showbiz types,' she claimed. Victoria was also reported to be seeing a local boy, Stuart Bilton, who lives and works near her parents' home. They have also since split up.

The clearest sign yet that the band had hit
the big time came when they were chosen to
switch on the Christmas lights in London's
Oxford Street – an honour only extended to
the most famous. They performed the ceremony from a platform outside the HMV
store in front of more than 5,000 cheering
fans on 7 November. For Victoria, it was the
moment that she realized just how big the
Spice Girls had become. 'We went through
these barriers and there were policemen and
security guards everywhere. We just drove
straight through. We looked at each other
and started squealing.'

Mel C was also amazed by the throng of
people all waiting to see them. 'But the next
day I went to Oxford Street to go shopping
and no one looked at me. When we're out
on our own, no one pays us any attention,'
she claimed.

In the same month as they switched on the
Christmas lights, the band also released their
debut album, *Spice*. Like everything else
associated with the Spice Girls, copies of the
album were cleared from the shelves as

quickly as the stores could stock them. It was announced that the band had become Japan's biggest-selling act since The Beatles. Not long afterwards, they picked up their first awards. In the *Smash Hits* poll, they were voted Best British Group, Best New Act, and Best Pop Video. They collected another five awards in a poll of readers conducted in *The Sun* newspaper.

It was not just the Spice Girls' music that was making headlines either. They created a stir during their appearance on the British breakfast television station, GMTV, when all five of them flustered presenter Eamonn Holmes by asking him for a kiss.

Girl Power even became involved in the world of politics after the band claimed in an interview that former British Prime Minister Margaret Thatcher was a role model. 'She was the first true Spice Girl,' claimed Geri, who even joked about standing as a candidate in the general election. Geri later revealed that Lady Thatcher had sent the band a Christmas card.

The group's Christmas hit was '2 Become

1'. But the girls delayed its release so that the charity single 'Knockin' on Heaven's Door', which commemorated the victims of the Dunblane gun massacre, stood a better chance of reaching number one. 'If anyone is going to beat us to the top spot we'd love it to be the children of Dunblane. We would happily settle for number two,' said Mel C.

Even this generous gesture did not prevent '2 Become 1' going on to be the Christmas number one however. By the end of 1996, the Spice Girls had gone from being complete unknowns to the biggest name in pop music. It was an achievement that all of them could scarcely comprehend. 'At the beginning of the year, we wanted it so bad and at the end of the year, we've got it,' said Geri. 'The next big deal is to hang on in there.'

The girls were all struck in different ways about how fame had changed their lives. Emma admitted: 'We've changed as a group of people. We've always been close, but now we're really, really tight because no one else has any idea of all the things that have happened to us, except us. We're like real sisters now. There's nothing we don't know about each other.'

Mel B added: 'Everyone would expect us to say the big difference is the money, but they forget it's a long time before you see any of that. I'd say that what's changed most is other people's attitudes to us.' Mel C thought that getting to see the world was the greatest transformation in her life. 'I never thought I'd get to travel,' she said. 'Not so long ago, it was a big deal for me to go to London. I ring home now and say, "I'm in Japan" or "We're just leaving New York", and it feels so strange as I say it.'

Even so, there were some disadvantages to being constantly in the public eye. Before the first success of 'Wannabe', Mel C had joined a women's football team in Rickmansworth, Hertfordshire, England, to indulge her greatest passion. But the demands of the Spice Girls' schedule meant she had been unable to turn out for the team. Instead she spent £2,000 on a new kit for the whole team, which had 'Spice Girls' and 'Virgin

Records' embroidered in red on the front.

Asked about the pressures of fame, Mel C replied: 'It has been brilliant because it's everything we ever dreamed of. But it never stops. Recently, we were filming a video and, at the same time, doing something for MTV (the pop music cable channel) and another interview. Victoria said: "I feel like screaming." I felt exactly the same.'

The girls' families noticed the change in their lives too. Mel B's mum, Andrea, said, 'Mel loves being in the band and it's great seeing her on telly. I am very proud of her and how hard she has worked over the years. The downside is that I do miss her a lot – but I suppose that's the price I have to pay for her success.'

Mel B herself illustrated the non-stop lifestyle of the girls. 'We get these schedules every day. On them is what we are doing every minute of the day, sometimes from six a.m. to midnight. You can't look at more than one at a time or you'd go mad.'

Geri agreed, but added: 'We can't complain. It's what we always wanted to do and we're having the time of our lives. The minute this stops being fun, we'll stop doing it. But at the moment, it's the best job in the world.'

At the beginning of 1997, the Spice Girls flew across the Atlantic Ocean to tackle their greatest challenge yet. The most successful acts in pop music history are those who can claim to have conquered America, and many bands have failed in the attempt, despite enjoying huge recognition in Britain and Europe.

Take That were the most recent example, and Oasis also struggled to make an impact in the USA at first. Much of the opinion in the music industry was that the Spice Girls would suffer a similar fate. But no sooner had they landed on American soil, than the girls were getting noticed.

For much of that they had MTV to thank. The video for 'Wannabe' had already gone to number one on the channel's play list before the band arrived, which meant that it was being seen by at least thirty million American teenagers. At the same time, the single was blaring out at least once an hour, every hour, on America's 100 biggest radio stations.

'We always wanted to be an international act, not just big in the UK,' said Mel C. 'When we arrived in America we didn't think anyone would have a clue who we were. But people here seem to be catching on very fast.' She added: 'Outside radio stations and hotels they keep singing "Wannabe" to us – but in American accents. It's really funny.'

The proof of the Spice Girls' effect upon America came when 'Wannabe' went straight in at number eleven in the country's top chart – the Billboard Hot 100. It was the highest entry ever by a British band in the USA – a feat which not even the legendary Beatles could manage with their first American hit, 'I Want To Hold Your Hand', which went into the same chart at only number twelve in 1964.

In its second week on the Billboard Hot 100, 'Wannabe' leapt to number six, and the following week it knocked Toni Braxton's 'Unbreak My Heart' off the number one spot. By now, 'Wannabe' had sold more than

700,000 copies in America, another boost to its enormous total worldwide sales. It was also the first number one by a British act in America for two years, and stayed there for four weeks.

In New York, the girls were the talk of the town. They were put up in a luxurious Manhattan hotel, where the rooms cost over £500 per night. Even though such stars as the German supermodel, Claudia Schiffer, and the actors Matthew Perry and David Schwimmer (better known as Chandler and Ross in the American comedy, *Friends*) were staying in the same hotel, they were practically ignored by the media and the fans who swarmed around the Spice Girls. In a van with blacked-out windows, they were ferried around the Big Apple, from a personal appearance one minute to yet another television interview the next. One New York critic claimed: 'They're going to be around for a long time to come.'

The circumstances could not have been more perfect for the release of the *Spice* album in America. During the band's stay there, it entered the American album charts at number six. Within a month, it had sold one million copies.

Almost inevitably, speculation began to grow that the band would move out to America permanently. However, Geri was quick to end the rumours. 'Now everyone is expecting us to up sticks and move over there for good, but we'd never do it,' she said. 'We love Britain too much and we're dead proud to be British.' Mel C's mum, Joan, also thought it was unlikely. 'There's no way they'll go. All the girls are far too close to their families,' she claimed.

As a sign of exactly how close the five girls were to their families, they dedicated 'Mama' – one half of their next single, along with 'Who Do You Think You Are?' – to their mothers, and even gave them a starring role in the video. Mel B said of her mum, Andrea: 'She really enjoyed it and it was great for her to see what we do for a living.' Geri, whose mum, Anna, was also in the video, said: 'It's a wonderful way to say thank you to the ones we love.'

By going straight to number one again with 'Who Do You Think You Are?'/'Mama', the Spice Girls had made history and underlined again their extraordinary popularity. At the beginning of April 1997, they notched up their ten-millionth sale of *Spice* worldwide. Added to the fourteen-million singles they had sold across the globe, it meant that all five girls were multi-millionaires. A spokesman for their record company, Virgin, commented: 'They are the biggest pop phenomenon of this decade, if not of the last twenty years.'

Most incredibly, they had achieved all this unprecedented success in less than twelve months. Now the question being asked by everyone was: what on earth was there left for the Spice Girls to do next?

CHAPTER NINE
The Future

Pop music can be a strange thing. One moment you are the biggest act in the business; the next, you are yesterday's pin-ups. Following their staggering recent achievements, the trick now for the Spice Girls is to remain on top.

Certainly there seems to be no end in sight to their success. The album *Spice* was reported at one point to be selling at the rate of up to 400,000 copies per week – and that was just in Britain. Their singles have now topped the charts in thirty-one countries. An official video featuring those first four number one singles won 500,000 orders in advance. A book written by the girls was translated into twenty different languages.

'The last big girl group was Bananarama and they were around for seven years. The Spice Girls have easily outsold them in their short career,' said a spokesman for their record company, Virgin. To give some idea of the impact that the band has made, Virgin also revealed that it expected to sell a maximum of only 300,000 copies of *Spice* in Britain when it first came out. 'We are already eight times that number in this country, and that is pretty much the scale of how amazed we have been.'

There has already been plenty of speculation about how wealthy the girls are now. The most authoritative estimate suggests that each of the five has a personal fortune of approximately £2.2 million – but with much more still to come. However, they have not noticed any great change so far as a result of owning all that money. Mel C says: 'We haven't seen any of the money yet. It takes forever to come through.'

That is not to say that the girls haven't been

able to buy and do things of which they could once only have dreamed. Mel B paid off the mortgage on her parents' house in Leeds after her father lost his job. 'It was my way of saying "Sorry I was such a brat when I was younger,"' Mel explained. She also bought a sporty convertible car for her mum, Andrea. 'Mel said she was going to meet her mum at a railway station and wanted to tell her to tear up her return ticket, then surprise her with the car,' said a stunned salesman at the car dealership afterwards.

Emma has also bought herself a car, but what she wants most of all is to be able to buy mum Pauline and brother Paul a new house, and then get a place of her own. 'I'd love to have a garden,' she says. Geri's biggest luxury so far has been a sports car with silver spokes, but she insists: 'I was just as happy when I was skint.' Victoria, meanwhile, was spotted in New York by Shellie and Karen from fellow girl band Alisha's Attic, laden down with bags of designer clothes from the Big Apple's most expensive stores. Back home, she was also seen out with

Manchester United and England footballer, David Beckham, her latest boyfriend.

Not surprisingly, some of the world's leading companies have been queuing up to persuade the Spice Girls to advertise their products. They filmed an advert for the giant soft drinks company, Pepsi, and also each of the girls was given a two-seater sports car plus £10,000 in cash by the German car makers, Mercedes, in return for them helping to unveil the latest Formula 1 McLaren racing car. The band was also involved on the night that Britain's latest television station, Channel 5, was launched. They recorded a modern version of the Sixties' hit song '5–4–3–2–1', to be the station's theme.

Even the royal family was keen on the Spice Girls' support. Perhaps acting on advice from his eldest son Prince William who, as we have seen, is a big fan, Prince Charles invited the band to top the bill at a royal gala in Manchester to raise funds for his charity, the Prince's Trust.

Having conquered the pop world, the girls now plan to break into the movies as well.

They will make their big screen debut in *Five*, a comedy adventure. The script for this has been written by comedienne and creator of *Absolutely Fabulous*, Jennifer Saunders. A soundtrack album from the film will be released in November, including five new songs, and *Five* itself will open in cinemas over Christmas.

But perhaps the greatest test of all for the Spice Girls will be the world concert tour that is scheduled to begin in February 1998. It promises to be a glittering spectacle, taking in the biggest cities across the world, and it is reported that it might be sponsored by Pepsi. It should also answer some critics who have claimed that the girls only mime to their songs on stage, an impression that they have already corrected by appearing live on the hugely popular American TV show, *Saturday Night Live*.

What is certain is that the girls will have little or no time to rest. The year ahead looks just as hectic as the last twelve months have been. But that is something that the world's top girl group are ready to face. Victoria says,

'Sometimes I lie in bed thinking I'm so tired that I can't possibly get up, but when I'm with the girls I feel fine again because we all pick up energy off each other.'

It is, typically, Geri who sums up the band's attitude to their non-stop work schedule. 'I'd rather die from exhaustion than boredom,' she says. 'There's never a moment when we're bored.'

For as long as the Spice Girls are around, there will never be a dull moment for their fans either.